DOWN WE GO &
OTHER STRANGE TALES:
An Anthology of Weird Flash Fiction

DOWN WE GO &
OTHER STRANGE TALES:
An Anthology of Weird Flash Fiction

MINUTE FICTION
VOLUME #1

Minute Fiction

ISBN-13: 978-1-7323323-0-0
ISBN: 1-7323323-0-0

Cover art: Raun Edano
Illustrations: Robin Edano and Raun Edano
Special thanks to Annette Corkey, Alex White and Sophia Lawhead

Printed in the United States of America
First Edition

TABLE OF CONTENTS

INTRODUCTION

Welcome to our anthology of weird flash fiction. Now, check your expectations at the (trap)door because we aren't here to categorize this book. Then why call it *weird?* Simply put, our brains like to group concepts into meaty, digestible chunks, and *weird* describes our collection in the best way. Being huge nerds, we loved sci-fi and fantasy; but as we worked, horror seeped in, dug a hole and made itself a home in our stories. The only sensible choice left was "weird fiction."

The classification of weird has a long history with many definitions that have evolved with time. Our take on the genre isn't entirely the traditional fare you'll find in works by H.P. Lovecraft, where characters stare into the abyss hoping it doesn't stare back (there aren't any tentacles in our anthology either, though one story with a space squid nearly made it in). We also don't fully fit in "new weird" with its grotesque, edgy, urban tales that have seen a resurgence in the last ten years thanks to China Mieville and Anne and Jeff VanderMeer. Yet our anthology straddles the boundaries of old and new weird. Stripped down to its barest bones, this book is a mishmash of horror, fantasy and speculative fiction, with weird bits of *"What the hell just happened?"*

Brevity is the other defining trait of our collection. The premise of flash is to create a complete story—beginning, middle, end, conflict, tension, emotion—all under a certain word limit. Depending on the publication, there are interchangeable word counts decreeing exactly what flash fiction is. For our part, we decided on a maximum of 1200 words. The genre was a hairy beast to conquer because in flash fiction, every single word must have its place. True, the same can be said of novels or short stories, but when confined to specific restrictions, the minute nature of flash requires precision and omission.

As a result, you won't find answers to every question in these tiny, weird stories, but there's plenty to keep you occupied. There are living nightmares in the shadows of space and the space of a young boy's mind. There's a woman facing the end of her story, and a man who wants a punishment to fit the crime. And there are forests, so many forests where you'll meet violently fierce protectors, escaped monsters and a mysterious set of stairs that might just drive you insane. But most of all, there's a strange darkness—whether it's familiar or foreign is up to you.

If you're perplexed so far, then consider us pleased. If you want to keep reading, consider us over the moon. My own personal hope is that you come away unsettled and satisfied with what we've tried to do—and perhaps you'll find yourself triple-checking the lock on your doors tonight.

PS: In the anthology *Unnatural Creatures*, Neil Gaiman notes that an introduction is not the place for acknowledgments, but sometimes, it's worth including to embarrass people who worked extremely hard on the book (and I love embarrassing people I care about).

That said, thank you to my fellow authors and editors, for without them, this project would not have existed. Thanks to Ashley Reed, Peter Corkey, Nicole Ellis, our layout expert Alex White and our wonderful proofreader Annette Corkey. Finally, thank you to Raun Edano and Robin Edano, our incredibly talented artists who brought our stories to life with beautiful illustrations.

From the bottom of my beating heart, thank you all.

Lily Prasuethsut
May 2018

THE INK WELLS

MARCH 30th IS COMING

The lights in her matchbox of an apartment are dim, but the ink reflects clearly on her skin all the same. Standing before the bathroom mirror, Nora studies the words stamped across her throat. She knows better than to try and scrub them out. If she's patient, they will fade on their own.

She finishes dressing, knots a short scarf around her neck for some semblance of security, and walks out the door to work. She tries to ignore the itch of the seeping ink under the cloth.

She works with words in an office, so maybe this is why they follow her around and bleed into her skin. She works in the office drafting documents she forgets as soon as she's done writing them. They have enough magic for the lamps and sending messages without postage, but not to do the paperwork.

Sometimes she thinks she spends too long staring at words, because when she looks up, the people around her can be read as books, with the prose hovering just above their skin. Some can be skimmed easily; others require a deeper perusal.

For instance, today there is a handsome boy that materializes at the center of the office. His skin is dense with descriptors, revealing *a mischief-maker, born to a mother of a respectable family; father is unknown and she never gave his name . . .*

He approaches Nora's desk, his smile charming, to talk about what a shame it is that her boss won't allow him access to a certain private document. He, a poor history student, desperately needs it, and, besides, *wouldn't she like a chance to discover a secret?*

Everything he says flows right into the other sentences she sees swirling around him. He doesn't seem real—she can't take him seriously at all. The conversation sputters and dies.

He leaves, and she stays at her desk until evening, closing herself off from the growing din in the streets that rattles the windows and hammers the inside of her skull.

The next day, it's a beautiful girl that enters her boss's office and talks to Nora about secret documents. The same scene repeats, right down to the evening furor.

Head aching, she slips out the back door to escape.

Each morning, she finds sentence fragments scrawled across every limb. Ink smudges on her clothes and sheets, though the words themselves remain clear.

Sometimes they are instructions.

. . . Follow the old cobblestone road to see the marching crowds . . .

Or aspirational.

Today is the day that things will change.

Change to what, she doesn't know. She begins to see the same writing throughout her neighborhood, splashed across the walls: some, false starts; others, dramatic phrases without payoff.

She used to think it was graffiti, some teenager with a melo-dramatic streak.

Now, she wonders.

The sentences are not fading as they usually would. Great chains of clauses now circle her abdomen. Shorthand and non-sensical notes mark up any spare inches. One morning, she finds lists of traits stamped down her legs:

EMPATHETIC
HAPPY
SHY

Are they supposed to be her?

The city grows tight with tension. She reads about strange events downtown, such as rumors of a new magic, or a day when a riot broke out and blood soaked the streets.

Sometimes her body starts to take heavy steps towards the turmoil, but she always changes her mind. It doesn't feel right.

As March 30th draws closer, she finds demands across her back.

WHAT ARE YOU DOING?
FOLLOW THE BEATS

Impulsively, childishly, she finds a marker of her own and writes a response across her forearm.

Let me figure it out

She watches the ink glisten, before her skin absorbs it. When she returns to the mirror, the orders have been wiped clean.

March 30th approaches, and her city changes. The buildings around her grow translucent. The insides of shops and homes are visible not just through windows, but the walls themselves, now blown-glass thin. The sky is bleached of color, as if shrouded in an eternal haze. It doesn't even shift from day to night.

For the first time, Nora looks for the source, wanting to find clues for the thinning of her corner of the world. She peers through her neighbors' apartments and down the flimsy streets. She skims her hand carefully over the walls, searching for anything off. She can't ask for help—her neighbors are now no more than moving outlines of words.

She finds it when she makes her way back to her apartment, once cold gray stone, but now the color of smoke and the texture of chalk. If she squints the right way, she can see a surprisingly solid figure behind it.

She reaches forward and touches her hand to the wall, which gives easily under the light pressure. Passing her hand over it, she finds cracks in the facade. She digs her fingers in and pries it back. The wall tears and shatters in her hands, exposing a black wound to the air.

She steps through.

At the center of the void, a woman sits at a desk, scribbling.

"Oh," she says, looking up when Nora approaches her. "*Now* you do something interesting."

This is her tormentor, this tired-looking woman with the frizzy sweater and bony wrists, stains on her fingers and an ink well at her elbow.

"Are you a witch?" Nora asks.

"No," says the woman. She taps a pen nib against the table, scoring the wood with the force. "You might be. Not that it would fit at this point, of course."

"That's not *my* fault," says Nora haughtily. "It all felt wrong. If I can see your words, you're not doing it right."

Nora rolls up her sleeves, exposing the false starts, scraps of characterization, and other notes that have been made over the last few months.

"You could have *tried*," complains the woman. "Just given them the answers they needed and joined the fray. I'm going to miss my deadline."

"March 30th." Nora crosses her arms tightly over her chest. "So? I need more time."

"Well, I don't have it. I have the others to salvage—*their* story should still make sense."

The woman shuffles the papers on her desk back together, takes up her pen, and begins to black out entire lines of script. Nora feels the sentences well up within her, like the heat of a fever. They bleed out into the fabric of her clothes, sticking everything together, twisting and forming great bands. She tears at them, panic rising, feeling herself unravel.

"I think I see it now," says the woman sadly, cutting words in great swathes. "You don't fit; you won't meet up with the others. Maybe another time."

"Just spend more time with me," pleads Nora.

"I don't have any to spare," says the woman. "You are not

right for this story."

Nora collapses. Ink weeps from her eyes, and the sentences across her skin bleed together and begin to seep, dissolving her. The woman watches until there is nothing. Then, taking her pen, she dips it into the well, to fill the new space.

TELANO

Leila flicked her burnt-down cigarette into the growing night, its glowing cherry disappearing off the side of the road. In the time it took her to reach for another, the engine blew. With a metallic groan, it dumped a cloud of smoke onto her windshield. Stacking up a clutter of swear words, she smacked the wheel until her hand stung and pulled onto the shoulder.

It was only when the car had chugged to a gravel-popping stop that she noticed the gas station. Just a few yards away, fluorescent lights droned over four antique-looking gas pumps. Scrubby desert trees huddled around a cracked parking lot. A weather-beaten "Welcome to Telano" sign swung gently in front of a "Fire Danger" placard. A neon sign danced "Open" across the convenience store window.

Slamming her door and stomping up to the store, she passed a

21

pack of teenagers sucking down troughs of soda on the half-painted bench outside. She could feel them watching her as she went by. Weirdos.

The store bell echoed hollowly over rows of candy bars and car supplies as she entered. "Hey," she called to a balding man in a faded orange uniform behind the counter. "My car's busted. Can you fix it or something? Is there a mechanic here?"

Head tilting up, the guy stared at her over a rack of sunflower seeds. He said nothing, but didn't look away, his gaze sharp. Leila shuffled back a step, eyes darting around the room.

"What?" she scoffed, but that didn't shake any words out of him. She snorted a "Fine, whatever," and wheeled on the door, grabbing a candy bar as she stormed out.

Her eyes stayed fixed on her car until she was in the driver's seat and locking the doors behind her. She glared at the weirdos yammering on the bench as she dialed AAA. At least this place had service.

A robot voice announced it was "triangulating your location" over her phone speaker. Great. She didn't even want to go on this damn camping trip, and now she was spending her Friday on a date with a tow truck. The "Welcome to Telano" sign swung in the wind, mocking her.

"Roadside Assistance: This is Jeana speaking. How may I help you?" came an annoyingly cheery voice.

"My engine's messed up," Leila said, leaning back and glancing at the station. The teenagers were gone, light flickering over the empty bench. Fingers of shadow curled around the dirty white brick wall. It made her realize how heavy the dark was now, creeping up on her car. She sank down in her seat. "Pretty sure I need a tow truck."

"I'm sorry to hear that, ma'am. Can you tell me where you're located? I'm afraid I can't geo-locate you."

"*Fine*. Uh . . ." Leila looked up at the swaying sign. "Telano, Oregon, I guess. Some gas station in the middle of nowhere."

"One moment, ma'am," Jeana said, her voice crackling with static. The soft clicking of computer keys filled the car, barely louder than the breeze outside. After a moment, it stopped. The line went quiet.

"Hello?" Leila snapped.

"Apologies, ma'am, did you say 'Telano'? T-E-L-A-N-O?"

"Yeah."

"Are you sure?"

"Wha—?" Leila squeaked. "No, I made it up. *Yeah, I'm sure!* I'm staring at the damn sign!"

As the last word rocketed out of her mouth, the sign swung back into the station's pale light. The paint was gone. The *name* was gone. Only a blackened, scorched piece of wood hung there now. She stammered, nearly dropping the phone.

"I'm sorry, ma'am," said Jeana. "It's just that my records say Telano—"

With a high-pitched *boop*, the call ended. The wind battered her car, whistling fiercely as she squawked and dialed again. "Call failed," the phone said—once, twice, three times, as she tried over and over.

"Fuck," she sobbed under her breath. "Fuck, fuck, *fuck!*" She flung the phone into the passenger's seat and snatched her cigarette pack, clicking her lighter with shaking fingers.

As she sucked in a lungful of calming smoke, she spotted the teenagers again. They were hovering around one of the gas pumps now. Still. Silent. Staring at her car.

She shifted away from the window, taking the deepest drag she could. Her phone *plinged* cheerfully.

"Telano," came its eerily bright voice. *The hell?* "Here's what I found: Telano is a ghost town in the northwestern United States, in Grant County, Oregon."

Ghost town. It rang in her ears, dodging her brain.

"Founded in 1873, it acted as a central rail hub for—" The voice jittered and scratched, like it had been overtaken by radio static. Leila stared at the phone, afraid to touch it. The screen flickered to life and the voice returned, but it was deeper, slower, labored. "The remaining structures in Telano were destroyed in the Dixie Fire in 1976, which killed 18 people. The town was not rebuilt."

A chill fought through the nicotine to race up her back. Slowly, her eyes pulled her head, twisting her toward the window.

The teenagers had moved. They stood only a few feet from her car. The balding clerk had emerged from the store, gaze locked on her. And she was sure, out of the corner of her eye, she saw shifting in the shadows behind the white-brick wall. Human shapes shuffled out of the dark.

A whimper slithering out of her mouth, Leila lunged for her

purse. Her keys slipped through her fingers like ice cubes. With a cry, she jammed the metal into the ignition and twisted. The engine whined pathetically, grunting as it struggled to start—

Leila screamed as something slammed against her car. The sedan rocked back and forth, shadows flailing outside, savage blows pounding the metal. A fist crashed against her window, and through her wail she saw a face leaning close—a face blistered angry red, melted down to scraps on white bone.

Leila's voice broke, her sobs silent and shredded. "Officials believe," the phone droned, "the fire was human-related, started by"—the voice warped into something venomous—"a cigarette thrown from a passing vehicle."

Fists beat the car all around her—some crooked, some wrinkled, one small enough to be a child's. She didn't notice the orange glow out her back window—crawling up from the edge of the road where her cigarette had landed—until there was nothing else to see. A scream ripped through Leila's throat as she scrambled back against the dashboard. "*No!*"

Embers spiraled around her car. Flames licked over the trunk, up onto the roof. Glass shattered beneath melting fists. Leila's scream lit on the wind and whirled into the night.

It was hours before the bright orange glow fizzled, cooling enough to let the dark settle back in. The wind calmed to a gentle breeze and a chorus of crickets filled the dry air.

In the morning, the blue light of dawn cast itself over scrub brush and the husk of a car on the side of the road, license plate burned clean away.

THE STOWAWAY

Good morning, Roscoe Dixon, Galactic Medical LLC.
Three new updates available.
First update: Location confirmed.
Time to weigh station and final destination: 0:44:06.

Rosco jolted to attention as the freighter's alert system pierced through the silence of the tiny cockpit and echoed through the ship. "Well, I'll be a son of a gun. You hear that, Kiwi? We're nearly home." His parakeet, perched in her cage above the co-pilot seat, chirped in excitement.

It had been five sleepless nights hurtling through space since his departure from the medical depot, and good news was exactly what he needed. His monthly trek to and from was always the same: Pick up the fresh-blood delivery at the depot per Company orders, break Company orders to rescue as many refugees from the planet as possible, then head home. Rinse and repeat.

The nightmares that haunted him whenever he dozed off were a side effect of the job. As if the years of exploitation that had left his people with nothing weren't enough, the rumors he heard of mutated horrors lurking the planet now occupied his mind: The creatures that preyed on his people drained their disease-curing blood to survive. In a way, AG127 had become a battleground for these once-human creatures and the Company that was profiting at his people's expense: Who would ultimately claim this precious blood as their own?

Roscoe shuddered and took a deep drag on his cigarette, recalling his desperate attempts as a young man to steal a ship for his family and flee the planet. But he had to stay focused on doing what others had done for him so long ago and help more people start a new life.

Second update: Blood tank #3 integrity compromised. Service required.

"Shit," Roscoe sighed, rubbing his bloodshot eyes. "Well, I guess that'll take my mind off all this," he said to Kiwi, as he looked around the cramped cockpit for his boots.

Third update: Stowaway detected onboard. Restrain per protocol 391 and submit incident report immediately.

"What?" Roscoe groaned in disbelief, and rose from his seat, upsetting the layer of sunflower seeds that blanketed the cabin floor. Kiwi startled and fluttered around her cage.

"I thought it was weird there wasn't anyone to bring back with us this trip. We've normally got refugees fighting for a spot. All right. Hold down the fort, gal," he said. "I'll go meet our new friend and get 'em settled. But first . . ." he trailed off as he knelt over the console. With a flurry of keystrokes and a few swigs of coffee, the system was hacked and the data wiped in minutes—no more record of the refugee.

As Roscoe headed for the door, Kiwi began chirping wildly.

"Easy, girl. I'll be back in a jiff." Crouching to avoid count-less systems and instruments, he headed to the back of the cramped cockpit, flung open the steel door next to his bunk, and descended to the level below.

In the narrow cargo bay, Roscoe stood before three rows of towering blood tanks that stretched into the darkness. Kiwi's er-ratic twittering was distant but still audible over the low hum of the ship. Listening carefully for any unfamiliar sounds, Roscoe pressed the bay's light panel on the wall closest to him, but the flickering bulbs overhead did little to brighten the space. Before he could take a step, Roscoe heard the faint patter of feet echo from the far end of the bay. An unwelcome chill shot down his spine.

"Hello?" he yelled, but only dripping sounds and Kiwi's chirps responded. "It's okay. I'm a friend. I helped the Albanes last month." Roscoe listened for a reply before trying again. "You know the Albanes?" No answer came. He walked slowly to the nearest row of blood tanks, finding the source of the drip: A tank had been punctured and a steady trail of blood was trickling down its side. Probably just got smacked during onboarding, Roscoe thought.

"All right, come on now. There ain't nothin' to be afraid of!" he yelled to the back of the room, then muttered, "Shit, maybe the sensors are on the fritz and there ain't nobody. Wouldn't be surprised." He took a deep breath and walked to the corner of the long room, past sealed loading doors that led out into the dark vacuum of space. He grabbed a rusted flashlight from a dusty shelf of tools. "Last call!" he yelled, before flipping the switch.

He dropped the flashlight the instant the beam shot on. In the split-second of light, Roscoe caught a glimpse of what looked like a thin gray withered arm as it retreated behind a wall of blood tanks.

"Shit!" he whispered to himself. Roscoe fumbled for the flashlight, but the bulb had shattered. *Get it together, man,* he thought. *You're seeing things. It's just some scared little kid or something.* He yelled out one more time. "H-hello?"

A *plink* followed by a loud clanging filled the room as several tools hit the floor. Roscoe whirled around—a tall gaunt shadow scurried out of the darkness toward the cockpit. It jolted past the loading doors and dim lights, briefly revealing a glistening humanoid form.

It was the last thing Roscoe saw before the lights went out.

30

The sound of the cockpit door locking filled the room. He could hear Kiwi chirping frantically, then a crash and silence. Roscoe stumbled his way through the darkness and pounded desperately on the hatch as his cries echoed through the cargo hold. The ship's alert system suddenly shot on and its mechanical voice blared into the hold:

New update: Storage bay loading doors online.
Stand clear—doors opening.

SHE WATCHES
SHE WAITS

The Victorian beauty stands out like a deep green emerald nestled in the middle of suburban stone. Massive ponderosa pines shield the sides from prying eyes. The scent of vanilla butterscotch pudding wafts through the window cracks whenever the wind ruffles the needles outside.

High ceilings rest on wide, ancient walls in the many rooms. Figuring out what hall goes where is a maze for the uninitiated. But trailing a hand on the kitchen wall can lead upstairs to the attic, or to the basement, or to forgotten alcoves.

The age of the house can be counted, like tree rings, from the layers of crinkled wallpaper underneath the coats of paint. The realtor had insisted they provided more insulation against drafts.

"They'll also help muffle sounds," he said, winking at the new-lyweds. He did not tell them the past owners had gone missing, rather "the mortgage on this whopper of a house was too much." But it was not his fault. He did not know what lies behind the walls.

His lewd comments and untruths did not stop them from signing the papers. And here they are, set on gutting this home, turning it into "a bed-and-breakfast." The fools think they will succeed.

"Honey?" Sally calls from the master bedroom. "Did you move my favorite earrings?" She brushes her dark blond hair out of her face with perfectly manicured nails. They look neon red against the burgundy wine she is holding. She is close, so close that the air smells of rotten grapes. It is nauseating.

"If they're the pinkish ones, then nope, haven't seen 'em," Jim yells from somewhere downstairs.

"'Pinkish'? They're not '*pink*,' Jim. They're expensive rose gold studs."

"I thought I was your favorite stud," Jim replies.

Sally sighs and then chuckles. She shuffles through the Chanel bottles and other delicate, colorful tubes on her vanity table. Then, halfheartedly, she rummages through a cardboard box.

Nearly three months after they moved in, there are still open containers everywhere. Half-filled with garish, glittery junk, none of these things will fit. They are too new, too shiny. Like Jim and Sally.

But already they are tired. There are so many little things going wrong in their little lives. The cat is missing. Their trinkets keep disappearing. They keep fighting.

An autumn wind drops needles across the roof shingles and the branches scrape against the windows. The sounds are soothing, like mice feet crawling all over the house. Sally has gone downstairs and does not hear the symphony.

Her second glass of wine is nearly empty. She has settled onto the couch against Jim's shoulder. He kisses the top of her head and says, "Maybe you haven't unpacked them yet?"

"I know I did . . . I swear I wore them to Patsy's dinner." She is swirling swill and tapping a socked foot on the coffee table.

"We still have a lot of boxes to look through," Jim says. "Unless the movers lost some. You know what? I think I'll call them in the morning and see . . ."

"But, Jim," Sally interrupts, "how could the movers lose my toothbrush? It was here a few nights ago. Did they come back to steal one used toothbrush?" Her sarcasm drips with venom. It is comical they are quarreling again so soon.

"Well, there are five bathrooms. Maybe you forgot which one you used it in, or maybe . . ." he trails off lamely. Jim is not a thinker. When the bickering starts, he shrinks away into himself.

"Or maybe I got bored with our gigantic two-sink master bathroom? That I went to the one downstairs in the back of the house because I wanted a tooth-brushing tour?"

"Christ, there's no need to get hostile, Sally."

But that is in her nature. Combative down to the bone. It will be pleasing to see the fight leave her.

"Well, there's no need to get stupid, Jim." They are now glaring at each other, much further apart on the couch.

"Stupid? You want to know what's stupid, Sally? Turning down the fridge temperature so it freezes. Do you like drinking frozen craft beer? Or frozen 2010 Chardonnay?"

My, my, he has some teeth after all.

"Jesus . . . I told you I didn't do that." She has started pacing now. He stands to match her stance and runs his hands through his dark brown hair. They look like monkeys in a cage, challenging each other for the last piece of fruit.

"I've turned the temperature up three times now."

"Well, it's an old house." Her tone is defiant, but she does not seem to fully believe herself.

"With new state-of-the-art appliances we just installed two weeks ago. There's no way, no *fucking* way, they could be breaking. I will sue the shit out of GE if they are." He mutters this last part and looks towards the kitchen.

Sally sighs. She seems tired from their repeated arguments. "Look, Jim, I'm sorry. Maybe it is the movers; I don't know." She sits back down and leans into the cushions. They are at the end of their rope, struggling to grasp at strands.

Jim lets out a long breath, as if counting to ten, then sits beside her. "I'm sorry, too, Sally," he says warily, grabbing her hand. "Repairing everything in the nooks and crannies by myself is taking its toll. I'm sure the paint fumes are driving you nuts, too. But it'll all be worth it when we open her up. We just have to figure out this mess."

There is still a small edge to her voice, like a butter knife, when she asks, "Have you noticed anything else is gone?"

"Now that I'm thinking about it, I couldn't find my sledge-hammer yesterday or any nails to hang up our new paintings. They should've been with the power tools."

Sally sits up slowly and asks, "Are you sure?"

"I'm pretty sure I checked all the boxes marked 'tools and supplies.'"

"Are you missing anything else? Because I can't find my sewing supplies anywhere. All the embroidery scissors, needles . . . it's like they just up and disappeared."

They sit, once again leaning against each other, murmuring about lost things. The wall panel slides open softly, shushing as dust coughs into the air from a year of idleness. Crouching low, I test each step like dipping my feet into a cold pool. The hammer hovers just above the lovely wooden floor. In my pockets, hand-fuls of nails plink against the scissors like a muffled wind chime.

Perhaps, finally, they will hear the sounds of the house. The aching creaks, the tired groans. The wind seeping through the lit-tle holes. The needles raining from the trees. These sounds bring me quiet ease, as I drift off to sleep, every night. There are ghosts in these walls. But I live here, too.

CHEF'S SPECIAL

She chewed slowly, mouth gummed up, barely able to swallow, as she watched specks of red rise out of a blanket of snow. From pinpricks they spread into heavy globs, growing together into a steaming crimson puddle.

She could only eye it for so long before she had to look away. Instead she stared into the fire, turning the meat skewer roasting over it. Had to get the cooking done while the wind was low and flames were holding.

The blob was spreading, fingers of bright liquid crawling across the ground. Overhead, the canyon walls stretched into the cloudy sky, insurmountable as ever. She guessed the sun was high above now, pale light catching in the fog. It wouldn't be another hour before it disappeared and the wind picked up again, careening through this chute of a ravine and eating at her bones.

She swallowed. The meat was cold and tasteless. She yearned for the industrial-sized buckets of salt and pepper in her kitchen aboard the ship, the only seasonings she'd had to flavor their meals as they spent weeks lugging minerals across the system. She used to complain about how much better her cooking could be with more spices. The thought made her mouth and eyes water.

The red glob stretched lazily around the fire, spreading into a semi-circle. More pinpricks started to emerge from the snow, lining up in tiny trails that led toward her camp from out of the fog. She looked up to avoid seeing them, staring at the bent, shredded port side of their ship. The rest of the vessel loomed behind her, broken, empty, half-buried, and cold. The noisy hum and clang of the engine had always gotten on her nerves, but the more its racket faded from memory, the more she missed it.

She refused to look out into the fog. They couldn't be angry. They would've done the same thing.

But now she wondered if she shouldn't have. There'd been nothing on the radio for weeks. She'd stopped chiseling slashes into the ship's rusting metal hull with her cooking knife a thousand frozen nights ago. The chirping distress beacon had gone unanswered for too long. No one was coming.

Viscous red slithered out of the mist, filling the grooves of four familiar trails before joining with the puddle. There was nothing for it—there was no ignoring the contorted shapes that stretched out of the slimy pool, looming over her fire.

She looked up, flinging a dry, ragged laugh at them. They all stood in front of her, lined up prim and proper like they always were before. The tall and stony captain, the lithe lieutenant, the freckle-faced engineer, the fashionable navigator—they stared with melting faces shaped by drippings of red. The paths ended at their feet, leading them all here, dragged back from where they'd been laid in the far-off mist.

Her laugh cracked as she choked on smoke. "Didn't wanna eat my *shit cooking* again anyway, did ya? Funny how things turn out."

She took another cold, sinewy bite. A shaft of light burst through the clouds.

Throwing her head back, she stared wide-eyed into a bright artificial glow that burned into her retinas as it grew. Behind it, she saw the dark gray of an interstellar cruiser descending into the canyon, its roar making her ears ring.

She shot up like a rocket, knocking the roasting meat from its perch. It tumbled through the ash and into the snow, melting through to the dirt underneath. Its fingers and palm steamed, blackened and blistered.

No. Shielding her eyes with a hand, she watched as the cruiser came closer, growing larger and larger. *No, no, no!*

The crew stared at her, oozing crimson and penning her in. In a moment, she would finally be rescued. And everyone would see what she'd done.

DOWN WE GO

Dec. 2

Dear E,

I went down the stairs today. Not too far. The wooden trap door felt heavier than before. The first step creaked; the second step sighed a chill down my spine. I was too chickenshit to keep going.

I didn't write you about it last time because I felt guilty breaking our promise. So here it fucking is: a letter of admission.

Sorry,

F

Dec. 10

Dear E,

Remember when T dragged us all over town to use her fancy new camcorder? Like that time she made us light twenty-two sparklers, a bottle rocket and a smoke bomb in the park?

I still can't believe she only got grounded for two weeks. Remember what she said? "It was an extremely important scene for a science fair project showing the extinction of dinosaurs" and "no one cared about the park until it burned up, anyway."

I'm smiling just thinking about it. T was crazy in the best ways. I hope it makes you laugh, too, and that you're not angry because I went down there again. Made it to step five this time. I swear something's at the bottom. Thought I'd write letters for you to find one day when I'm gone.

Yours,

F

Dec. 23

Dear E,

It's almost Christmas. It's always hard this time of year. I miss you. I miss all of us. We were so great together. You even kissed my cheek once. In retrospect, it was sweet—though confusing, since I always thought you loved T. She was the cooler twin. The one who could make anyone love her before they even knew her name.

Now, the house is empty; the streets are quiet. Snow is starting to blanket the dead trees. I don't leave much anymore, except to trudge back to the woods where the stairs are.

I miss her so damn much.

I'm going back tomorrow. I've already broken our promise. And it's not like you're around to talk me out of this.

Happy holidays,

F

Feb. 8

Dear E,

It's been a while since I've written to you. I almost wrote "talked," because this feels like talking. But it's been years since we've actually spoken. Maybe 20, but who's counting, right?

You all moved away, yet here I am, in the same old place. Do you ever feel it calling you? Have you woken up in the night wondering if you're in the right world? I hope not. I hope you're happy.

It felt like we would never be happy again after that night. So many things went wrong. No one looked at me the same afterwards. I was the kid without a sister. The kid who got lucky. The kid you didn't make eye contact with anymore.

Always,

F

Feb. 12

Almost went all the way down today because why the hell not? Then I remembered why. When I was running back up the steps, there was a wisp of a breeze that smelled like cinnamon apples and wet pennies. It called to me. Can you feel it?

Feb. 13

I lied. It was my fault. I should have known. She was my best friend, my sister.

The stairs tricked us. I know they did. I've set up a tent by the entrance to watch. It's cold, so cold, but the fire I've built helps, and something is bound to happen soon. The thought of that warms me the most.

The metal ring on the trap door is icy. Sometimes, I lift the door to make sure it doesn't freeze into the hard ground. You know what's funny? When we were younger, we never noticed any grass or trees by the door. It's still like that today. Nature knew to keep away, but we were too young and stupid to pay attention.

You probably think I'm insane, camping out in the woods during winter, but I hear it. Can you?

Feb. 14

Happy Valentine's Day, E. I've always loved you.

Remember our last Valentine's together, when T created a world that was made of marshmallows and we bounced all over the place scooping bits up to throw at each other? She was so powerful, we could actually taste the sweet goop sticking to our teeth. And remember how she made us squishy igloos with sugar-glass ceilings and we looked out into a magenta night sky speckled with swirls of purple cotton candy? You held my hand and everything felt right. I think she shaped that world just for us because we're allergic to chocolate and bullshit.

It was the last gift she gave us.

Feb. 15

My dearest E,

I figured it out, and I'm going to find her.

That night, when the walls were closing in and the breath was being sucked from our lungs, and we were crawling up each step, there was a sliver of a moment where T remembered how much we loved her and that we only said she shouldn't go down the stairs alone because we were worried. I can still see her furrowed brow when we begged her to escape with us. But we didn't know

48

we were already too late. I can still see her fading away, glassy and shiny like she was behind a window looking at strangers.

We were being punished for trying to take her away. We tried to bring her home when we should have gone with her. All this time, we could have been together.

Well, I'm ready now.

It's why the stairs have been acting up again, why I hear her voice whispering.

This time, the stairs can keep me. They know it, too.

I'm only sorry I didn't think of this sooner and that I never got to see you one last time. But it's okay. You'll learn to let go, just like me. You'll come back and find my letters. And then the stairs will keep you, too.

See you soon,

F

FAIR GAME

It's March when Basil "Bo" Blanchard's pickup rolls to a stop on a deserted forest road, the barrel of a hunting rifle peering out of his passenger-side window. Bear season has been over for months. But it's never stopped him before.

A crack explodes through the shadowy oaks and dogwood trees. Beside a creek thirty yards into the forest shade, a small black bear collapses with a muted groan. Its organs will sell for a high price—he's been in business long enough to know. Backing his truck into the forest as far as it can go, he leaves it idling and pulls a thick sheet of metal from the bed to use as a ramp. He descends on his kill with a long loop of rope, swiftly tying up the corpse.

Firing from a vehicle. Hunting out of season. Intent to sell. A history of disregard for the law.

This was his last strike.

It's only when he's dragged the still-warm body into the truck bed and tied it down tight that he notices the engine's gone silent. He swears under his breath and slams the tailgate shut, but when he walks around to the cab, he freezes midstep. He stares at something that he can't understand: Green vines thick as his forearm stretch from the ground, up the front of his truck, bending the edges of his hood where they've jammed beneath it. A carpet of lichen covers the roof and the windows. Thin, fibrous roots weave around the tires like a cocoon.

"The hell?" he mutters, and blinks, like he's touched some poison that's making him see things. Gingerly, he grips the edge of the hood and pulls up. It opens without resistance, revealing a tangled knot of vines that had, until a moment ago, been his engine.

Bo looks at it for a long time, then lets the hood drift closed and shuffles back into the driver's seat. Turning the key, he gets nothing in return—not the faintest click. He turns it harder, harder, *harder*, until he's grunting with the effort and the key groans like it'll snap in the ignition. Nothing. Behind him the sun is sinking fast, spreading a last golden shine on the dead bear's body as it ducks behind the trees.

He'll hitchhike, he's certainly thinking as he numbly retrieves his keys. Get back to town and find a tow truck to help him deal with—*this*. "Piece of shit," he curses, eyes fixed pointedly on the road and away from the mass of vines as he walks past.

By the time he notices the deep snorts and guttural roars in the bushes, they're too close to miss. Two barrel-shaped knots of muscle and fur lumber out of the brush, blocking his path. He freezes on the spot, his blood surely running cold. The massive brown bears grunt, agitated and full of teeth.

Shivering, he slowly backs up toward the truck and the gun inside. His eyes stay locked on the animals as he grabs the door handle and pulls. It doesn't budge. Only then does he notice the vines that have punctured the cab and shattered the window, chaining the door closed with links of green.

The underbrush disappears into the crawling gray of night as the sun's last dreary light shrinks away. Somewhere in the mire, death roars and stampedes toward him. Bo yowls in fear and abandons the door, making a desperate leap for the truck bed. Teeth close around his ankle and pull him down.

Laurie finally blinks through her own eyes at a map of California and pages of computer-printed hunting schedules on the wall. She cradles her head with a hiss. Always stings like a motherfucker.

Chris chuckles, taking his feet off his desk and adjusting his forest-green baseball cap. He knows without her saying anything. "Coffee's fresh, if you want some."

With a sigh, she shrugs on her heavy work jacket. The blue and yellow Department of Fish and Wildlife patch on the sleeve is suddenly so bright, she swears it's giving her a migraine. As she feels the green disappear from her eyes and her sense of smell fades back in, that warm, inviting bean-water scent fills their cabin. The coffee they get always tastes like mud, but it'll wash the tang of phantom blood off her teeth.

"You get 'im?" Chris asks as she wraps her hands around a full mug. "Ranger Mom" peeks between her fingers.

"Yep," she says. She drifts back into her chair, looking out the wide front window of their tower. Night's settled in, but light pours out through the glass like a waterfall that splashes to the ground below, over thick oaks and redwoods before fading into the dark. She can feel the rustle of rabbits in the leaves tapping across her skin, the swaying of the trees shifting in her hair, damp earth cushioning her feet and ivy wrapping like sleeves around her arms. Delicate drops of water start to bounce off the window.

"You'd think they'd learn," Chris yawns, setting down a paperback with *The New Druids* printed on the cover. Laurie doesn't have to look at him to know his eyes have turned a dark green around pupils of white.

"Wishful thinking," she says, and closes her eyes, feeling the rain on her skin.

THE BOG

With every step the young boy took, the gathering dark of the vast marshland seemed to close in around him. The setting sun cast dull orange beams past hanging moss and gnarled branches. He had his thoughts and despair to keep him company, but even without them he was not alone: Among the sparse oaks and cottonwoods, strange things slithered and peeked from behind every shadow. Black shimmering things that he struggled to ignore.

The boy had attempted this same journey almost a year ago now, and as he left the village at dawn, the parting words of his neighbors ensured he would not forget it. *The medicine woman will only speak with you, Dalton. You're the only family she has left. But you must hurry. You let your mother die and you better not let your sister die, too.*

The boy sniveled as he prodded the thick mud ahead of him

with a stick to gauge its depth. Rotting earthen fumes bubbled up from the shin-deep muck that slurped at his hide boots with every step. His progress through the misty swamp had come to a crawl, and Dalton knew the things in the shadows welcomed the hindrance.

Everyone's right, though, Dalton thought as he trudged on, stabbing at the mud. *Maybe they shouldn't have come looking for me. If I hadn't gotten lost in the swamp, I could have gotten to Aunt Morta's in time. I could have gotten the leeches that would have rid Momma of her sick blood and saved her from the bad thoughts. But I didn't.*

Dalton was never alone again after his mother died. Her voice was always whispering cruel words in his head, and things that seethed and lurked in the shadows watched him constantly. But they never showed themselves completely.

The boy wiped at misty eyes as he took a deep breath. His mother said she'd forgive him if he could save his sister from the curse in her mind: *I'll get the leeches this time, Momma. I'll be brave so she can live and you can leave me alone.*

Dalton's thoughts went quiet as he noticed the ground beneath his stick harden. The thick mire was giving way to solid earth. Up ahead, through a blanketing haze, trees and dried bramble began to envelope the barren mudflats. He breathed a sigh of relief. The old bramble thicket meant Aunt Morta's was close.

The things in the shadows were eager for solid ground, too. Among the thick woodland gloom, their grotesque wriggling forms crept through the underbrush and further into his mind.

56

As Dalton's pace quickened over the hard-packed earth, their crashing and slinking in the dark filled his ears, making his skin crawl. The sounds were familiar. He had grown accustomed to them since his mother died. But instead of feeling like a distant dream, they were louder and sharper and more real than before.

He hurried on, his heart pounding and legs aching as he shoved bramble and bush aside, hoping to find Aunt Morta's hovel. Dark, twisting forms appeared on either side of him, gliding through the thicket and keeping pace, closing in with his every step. He kept his eyes fixed on the path ahead. His lungs burned and his legs fumbled, and he knew he would not be able to handle the sight of them.

The sound of the shapes crashing through the heavy brush drowned out Dalton's footsteps as he broke through the last of the briar. His mud-caked boots suddenly found deep, moist earth and he stumbled to the ground. Gulping for air, he struggled to stand up. The old medicine woman's weathered shanty was close enough that he could hit it with a stone. But the sinuous, glistening blobs of flesh slithered out of the briar, blocking the path to the hut. The mucus from their black flesh trailed on the earth as they encircled him.

Dalton would have screamed if he could, but his heart stopped before he had a chance.

It was sun-up before the woman saw the boy's body in the moorlands just outside her window. She drew back a torn and tattered curtain, revealing his pale, lifeless form in the morning light. His tiny body showed no signs of a struggle.

"Another feeble mind, sick just like his mother and sister," she whispered to herself, holding a bowl of blood-filled leeches. *But this family's minds betray us all sooner or later.*

She turned to eye the dark undulating shape in the corner of the room. *And soon mine will too.*

STREETWALKERS

Kye almost spilled his drink when two quick knocks rapped across his door. He downed the cheap whiskey before his twitching fingers could shake it out of the glass. Shit. There it was.

The knocks came again, sharp and impatient. "Hold on!" he shouted, putting his foot through a small monument of takeout containers as he hustled toward the door. He pulled it open and *she* filled the frame—torn stockings, a cotton-candy-colored jacket longer than her dress and smoky eyes that peered at him through fluffy blonde hair.

He wasn't sure what was happening on his face, but when a sneer crawled across her lips, he guessed it wasn't good. "I don't think you're in a position to be picky, sweetheart."

"Sorry," he blurted. "I just—I guess I expected something different."

"Let me in and I'll slip into something more comfortable," she sighed. Without waiting, she brushed past him and flowed into the room.

He twitched as she sashayed into a circle of screens blasting blue-white light across dirty clothes and fossilized plates of food. As he closed the door, he could suddenly feel the patchy beard crawling out of his face and the grime on his skin. Fuck, when was the last time he showered?

"How about this?" she asked, her face catching the light. Her hair was short and red now, and her dress had transformed into a tank top and shorts. "Or . . ." Her skin shivered off her face as a thousand minuscule plates cascaded down her body. Soon it was a square-jawed man standing in Kye's living room instead. "Is this more your speed?" she—he?—said in an uncomfortably deep voice.

"No," Kye babbled, a full-body flush roasting his skin. "Just . . . that's fine, the second one's fine."

With a shrug, her female form fluttered back into place, and she stepped over a pile of mystery garbage to inspect the monitors. "Hmm. Hacker, right?"

He winced. "Keep your voice down, please."

"Right." She changed course and peered into his tiny bedroom. "You must be pretty good. The Collective's not known for their generosity. If they're paying this much, they like you."

"Yeah," he said distantly, gazing at the sea of code on those blazing screens. It'd been so long since he'd dropped into the net. The neural port in his temple itched. He wanted to plug in, feel the tickle of electricity in his head as he dove into data others thought they hid so well. He could just—

Reality blasted through his mind like a short circuit. It wouldn't let him go. "I'm Kye," he said abruptly, grasping for something else to think. Not that it mattered—not for this—but it felt normal.

"I know," she answered indifferently.

"And your name is . . ."

"Irrelevant."

"I mean, I feel like I should know who you are before"—he fumbled the words on a clumsy tongue, then gestured uncomfortably between them—"this happens."

"What a romantic."

"Look," he groaned, "I've never done this before. I don't know the protocol."

"I can tell, sweetie. I promise I'll be gentle. And we should get started, by the way."

A suffocating wave washed over him. This was really about to happen. Fuck, he should send her away. He didn't want this. He could just—just . . .

Nothing. He ran quaking hands over his face. He could just *nothing*. He didn't have a choice.

The room was empty when he looked up. Numbly he trudged through the electric blue air to the bedroom. He found her perched on his bed and fiddling with an earring, her face painted with streaks of gold shining through the blinds.

"So, here's how this works," she said as he sank to the

mattress. She gave the earring a twist and a pull, drawing a long, thin cord out of her ear. "You've hooked up before, right?"

"Not with another"—his eyes trailed over her hip, along the curve of her shoulder to her face—"person."

"Well, it's easy." She grabbed his hand and led it to the cord. "Just like logging on to the net. Except instead of ending up on the servers you land in here." She tapped her head with a perfectly manicured finger.

"So that's it," he said mechanically. "So we just—we hook up and then I'm—I'm inside you."

She shrugged. "That's about the size of it."

Dropping the cord like a live wire, he jumped up and paced from one wall to the other. "It's a data transfer, right?" he trilled, rubbing his face like he was trying to scrape off his skin. "What if you lose some pieces? What if you *delete* me?"

"Calm down," she said, twirling the cord absently. "It's lossless. I've cordoned off a section for you, too—our personalities can't cross the barrier. And I'm not going to delete you."

"So," he breathed, "I'm just some data floating around in your head . . ."

"And then the special protocol kicks in and I disconnect with you still stored. I'll walk out of here without a soul noticing, and in a few hours you'll wake up in a shiny new android body," she said nonchalantly. "No network signal to track you. You'll be home free."

He was going to be sick. His knees jellied, and he barely caught himself against the wall. *Android.*

"Look, I get you might be having trouble with this, but we have to move," she sighed, glancing at a bit of blue light on her wrist. "I didn't want to freak you out, but a van pulled up across the street just as I came in. I'd guess we have about ten minutes before they bust in here, and I've still got to make this look convincing."

He had just enough sense to throw up on the wall instead of her knees.

"Easy," she scoffed.

"I need to know, okay?" he shouted. "I'm losing everything. My life, my friends, and I just—and now I'm not even gonna be a person anymore. I'm gonna be this, this *thing* and like—will I still be *me?*"

Silence wrapped itself around the room. He'd never felt more alone, and it might be the last thing he ever felt.

"You'll be different." Her voice was even, a soft yet solid sound that spread up the walls. "But not because a robot messed you up. You don't walk away from this kind of thing and stay the same. But you'll be alive. That counts for something, right?"

He looked up as she reached forward and took his hand, guiding him back to the bed. He didn't take his eyes off her as she put the end of the cord to his temple, plugging into his neural port.

She pulled back and sat up straight, closing her eyes. "Ready?" It finally hit him how real she looked—just like any human. Realer even, maybe.

She cleared her throat. "Yeah," he muttered. Her skin was warm, and he found himself leaning closer.

"It's Jex, by the way," she said as he closed his eyes too.

"Ah." It was nice to hear. Strangely. "Cool. It'd be weird not knowing my roommate's name."

The last thing he heard for a long time was the sound of her laugh bouncing off the walls.

WATCH THE TEETH

When her mother brought home the new purse, Zara hated it at once. Its skin was textured like a crocodile's belly, dyed a poisonous crimson, and it had a zipper with long, needle-like teeth.

Her mother wore its strap across her chest like a bandolier. The weight would cut a faint red line into her neck. Zara had nightmares that one day the purse strap would draw itself tight and cut her mother's head clean off.

Then there was the fact that her mother never left it out at night. Instead, it went into the downstairs closet.

"Mom, what's in your purse?"

"It's just worth a lot of money," she would reply vaguely. "I don't want anything to get it. Don't worry; it won't be here for long."

Zara was no longer allowed to go downstairs after bedtime. Not after their dog got into a fight.

They had heard scratching and thuds and Roger's whimpers in the middle of the night, not long after the purse came. Her mother ran downstairs to find him cowering behind the sofa, scratched up and with a bloody nose. Her mother said a raccoon had gotten in. They boarded up the doggy door, but Roger was still skittish and couldn't be left downstairs alone.

That was when her mother started using the safe.

"You never know who could get in," she said.

Even with Roger upstairs, curled protectively at the foot of her bed, Zara could still hear something shuffling downstairs, rattling against the closet door.

Once, she caught the purse yawning on the kitchen table, its mouth stretched wide. Its hinges creaked with the strain, almost like a boa constrictor ready to devour its prey. Except, unlike a boa constrictor, it had teeth.

The weeks went by, and the purse did not leave.

By October, Zara circumnavigated any room where the purse resided, keeping near the walls and out of striking range. Her mother continued to feed it with keys and notes and lipstick, oblivious to its girth. It seemed to swell with all the things it knew.

66

Zara stayed out of sight as much as she could and waited for its moment of weakness.

School had started, and Zara walked home alone. Her mother was gone in the afternoons and had given her the alarm code to let herself in. With the purse out of the house, Zara was free to walk around without fear of ambush. A few days into her new freedom, she went back to the closet to look at the safe.

The code for the alarm was the same as the password for the family computer, and one they had used on other occasions.

That night, when it was far past her bedtime, Zara crept downstairs and opened the closet door. The safe looked as it always did, sturdy and unassuming, even with the purse inside.

Hands trembling, she tapped in the combination. Then, armored in oven mitts, she opened the safe.

She didn't wait to see if the purse would move; she grabbed it and ran, pinching its mouth closed as tightly as she could.

She stumbled through the backyard, past the fence that separated property from the open woods, and threw the purse as far as she could. It landed with a crunch, the thud softened by leaves.

She waited, listening, heart in her mouth. When she heard nothing, she returned to the house, finally able to breathe.

The porch lights were on. Zara froze but then forced herself to move forward.

"Zara." Her mother was waiting in the kitchen, the lines around her mouth drawn tight. "Where is my purse?"

"I don't know," she lied.

"This isn't funny, Zara."

"I mean it; *I don't know*," said Zara, flushing. She wondered if she should have searched the purse before throwing it away.

But her mother was already running, out of the house and back into the woods.

The black skeletons of the trees were cast in sharp relief against the darkening sky. Zara trailed after her mother, watching as she rushed towards the forest. At the roots of the largest oak was a strange lump, covered in dried brown leaves.

Her mother threw herself at the tree's roots, tearing away the detritus and digging deep gouges in the dirt. Zara hung a few steps back, hugging herself against the cold, until she heard her mother curse.

She was kneeling in the pool of leaves, clutching the bag with both hands. It was open but no longer looked like a mouth. The zipper's metal teeth were crooked, and the lining was torn.

"It escaped," said her mother. Her hands were shaking.

The forest seemed much louder. Zara heard a faint creaking in the wind, and the crunch of something shuffling over the leaves behind them.

BLOOD IN THE SNOW

As the flames of the campfire whipped about in the violet-dusk wind, Gudrun stared through the whirl of falling snow at the fiercest man in his service. With a cloak of pelts and his sprawling bronze beard, Torunn looked like a frost-covered grizzly.

"Are your hunters going to smoke the demons out of that damned cave so I can spill their blood, or are they going to make me suffer you until the end days?" the giant man bellowed when he caught Gudrun's stare.

Ignoring the mockery, Gudrun kept his gaze. The flames reminded Gudrun of the fire he had seen in the warrior's eyes the night Torunn lost his family, and it was there again now. "I understand you bear no love for our gods after what happened. But *my* hunting gods, and those of my people, can still punish us all the same. We can rid our village of the threat these beasts pose, but, monster or not, I urge you to remember that you'll doom us all if you slay their young."

Torunn spat. "You can offer *that* to your gods. We're slaying demons, not children. Your gods and these monsters have stolen my family from me, but I still have my axe. I'll make you no promises other than blood will be paid with blood before the sun has set." Torunn eyed his great-axe, deeply embedded in a nearby pine.

"Don't be hasty, Torunn," Gudrun said, rubbing his grey beard. "We have heard only rumors of these beasts. I want to confirm these sightings first. For all we know, these demons may be no more than–" Before he could finish speaking, Torunn's shout filled the air.

"You're a damned fool, Gudrun. It's these monsters that killed my wife and boy!" the man roared, rising from his place by the fire as Gudrun slowly felt for the knife at his side.

After a moment, Torunn turned away, the heaving of his chest slowing. "I'm the only warrior you have amongst your sheep herders and squirrel hunters. Bore me with this again, and it won't just be demons I'll be slaying."

Gudrun thought to curse the man, but bit his tongue. The man towered over him, and his fighting skills were unmatched. He needed Torunn in case the beasts were as monstrous as the tales claimed them to be. But Gudrun knew that cooler heads were needed if they were to succeed.

The old lord's eyes returned to the fire. Torunn had never

come to terms with his wife and child abandoning him. Gudrun and his village hadn't been able to calm his delusions or his need to place blame wherever he saw fit. A madman believes what he must to bury his grief.

The bitter cold was beginning to cut through Gudrun's fur cloak. He inched closer to the small campfire, rubbing his hide-covered hands for warmth, when Torunn suddenly leaped up, peering east through the pine grove that concealed them.

"Looks like your peasants finally managed to do something right."

Gudrun stood, struggling to see through the whirling blizzard to the mountainside not fifty yards ahead. The sheer rock wall was riddled with cave entrances like a massive stone beehive. He could just barely see one of his hunters at the mouth of a cave atop the ridge. Smoke was beginning to billow from the opening.

Through the thick snowfall, black forms emerged. The largest among them was no bigger than a man. The misshapen, dark-furred beasts shambled on two legs onto the field like lame animals, fleeing for the forest. Gudrun sighed in relief. Clearly the hearsay of their ferocity had been just that.

Without warning, Torunn reached for his axe and bolted for the clearing, crashing through the snow-covered forest like a rabid boar.

"Torunn, heed my words!" he yelled, but all that remained was the man's trail in the snow. Gudrun kicked out the fire and grabbed his bow, muttering a desperate prayer for forgiveness for what he feared the fool was about to do.

When Gudrun emerged from the pine grove, he could barely see a thing through the rising snowstorm and dim light of evening. The whipping haze of white ahead was riddled with dark shapes retreating toward the woods. Gudrun could just make out Torunn's massive silhouette as he reached the first of the beasts, his mighty axe nearly severing it in half. In the distance, a creature led a group of three small ones away from the fray. They would soon find the northern valley wall hidden in the blizzard's shroud, barring their escape. There was nowhere to run.

As Gudrun dashed forward, he saw Torunn cutting down more fleeing beasts, the north slopes a backdrop to his frenzy. The monsters limped away making no attempts to defend themselves against Torunn. Gudrun eyed the trail of the fallen as he ran past, but the blood-soaked piles of fur revealed nothing about the strange beasts. They looked no different than butchered deer after a hunt.

When Gudrun finally reached the valley wall, only three young beasts remained alive, struggling to climb the cliff face to safety. Torunn had them cornered in a whirl of wind, snow and ice. He lifted his axe high, poised to strike.

"These are no demons, Torunn, just frightened animals. Leave them!" Gudrun shouted.

Hope fell over him as he saw the man's weapon slowly drop. As Gudrun carefully stepped closer, an odd shape caught his eye.

At his feet lay a corpse. Amongst its bloodied furs, covered in ulcers and lesions, he could see a pale human hand.

Torunn's roar echoed through the storm. "Only blood can pay for blood!"

The giant rushed forward, weapon raised.

"Torunn, no!"

But it was too late. In one fell swoop, Torunn's great-axe struck the children down, their small bodies collapsing in the snow.

A sudden silence fell over the valley and the wind seemed to die with their last breaths. "I'm still here, old man." Torunn laughed facing Gudrun triumphantly. "Your gods don't care."

The last light of dusk vanished into an unnatural darkness. A rumbling high in the heavens began.

The flash of light that filled Gudrun's vision was the most beautiful thing he ever saw—and the last.

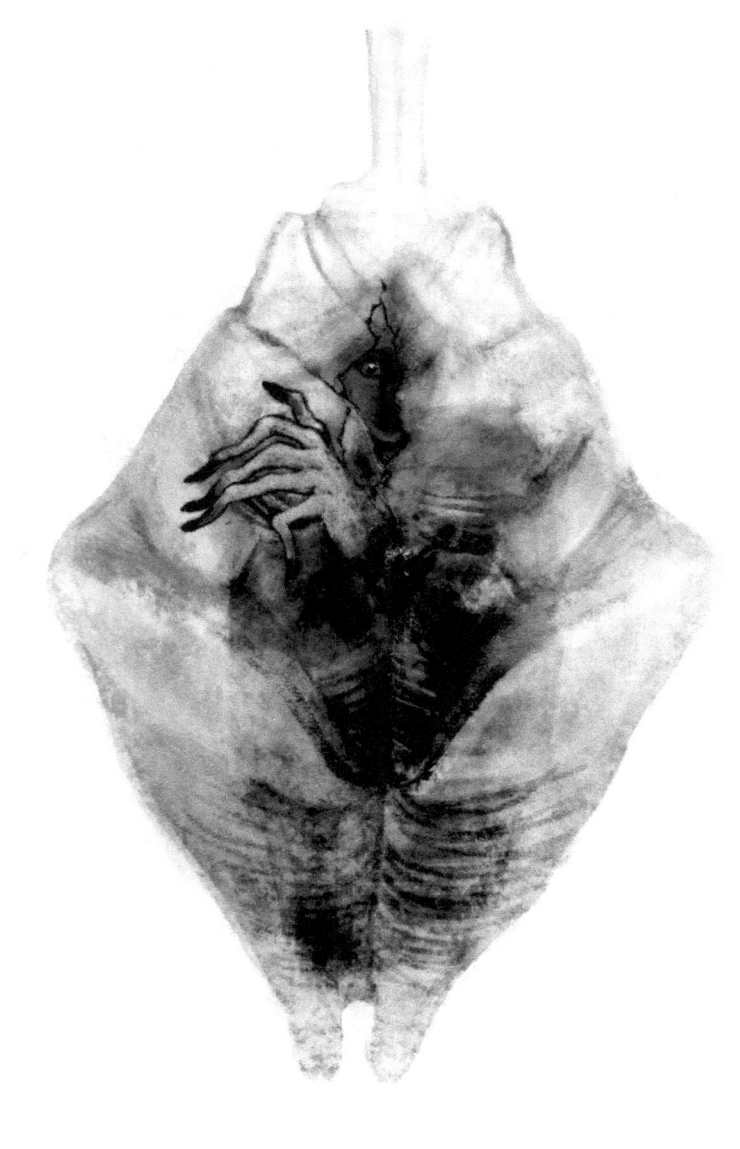

LONG LIVE THE QUEEN

Ninphor's fingers were not her own as she clawed at the inside of the cocoon. They were longer. An extra joint made them twist and curl strangely. They could not even grab the scabbard glued to her ribs with jelly. They had—*changed*. She buried the thought as the cocoon's inner shell stretched and groaned under her rending hands.

She could not think about it. Not now. She had to get out.

A fingertip caught on a miniscule gap in the membrane. Ninphor punched through and her hand grew heavy, shivering off globs of jelly in empty space. *Air*. She plunged her other arm into the gap—with a meaty *rip* the outer carapace split, and she tumbled into the open.

Tightly closed eyes saved her from the blinding light, but she could not hide from the noise. Her ears rang with the sound of a thousand murmurs shimmering through the air. Free of the cocoon's suffocating skin, she shivered on the sandy ground like a newborn, and the arms she wrapped around herself were too gangly and alien. Was this how every queen felt?

No. Move! With an agonized yell Ninphor forced herself onto her knees, dragging her atrophied legs. Her eyes watered as she tilted her head back, gazing at the sheer rock walls that surrounded her. Bioluminescent moss stretched across the stone, growing in the path of trickling water. She could just make out dozens—no, hundreds of craning heads, peering at her from gaps carved in the rock.

They grew quiet. She was the first. Ninphor's muscles tensed, and with a groan she dragged herself upright. Her knees didn't give way, and her ankles held. The royal jelly was doing its work.

Five cocoons hung behind her like monuments, clinging to stalactites with fibrous tendrils. Her own swathe lay open and dissolved like a collapsed air bladder, but the rest were untouched, the other potential queens still asleep inside. Then a hint of movement caught her eye: a shadow writhed inside the middle pod, the hull straining and cracking as the one inside tried to force her way out.

Ninphor's hand fell to her side as she limped toward the cocoon. The ceremonial knife and sheath were still there. Now that she could grip the hilt, the metal slid free without a hint of resistance. Gently, she rested a hand on the carapace.

A wail shivered through the blade as she plunged it into the flesh.

Lydele dreamed of the old queen. The colony assembled around the elegant monarch, heads tilted back as she towered over them. Her eyes were foggy, her blue-green skin pale and paper-thin. She barely had strength for the choosing.

But with impossibly long fingers she pointed at Lydele.

Now, as Lydele woke squirming in the confines of her pod, she could see the thrashing of dark shapes through its slippery flesh. Muffled shrieks seeped in, turning her insides to stone.

No. No no no the others were free.

She couldn't breathe. Thick jelly choked her, stifling her sob as the cocoon's membrane slid away from every scrape and scratch.

She didn't want to die. Not in here.

Something pulled tight around her chest as she tried to shout—a leather strap. *Her knife!* She clumsily snatched the hilt at her side and slashed as hard as she could, hacking through the sticky film. The cocoon tore open and she toppled to the ground.

At first all she saw outside were flailing, deep blue shapes—then they sharpened into grappling fighters, all younger reflections of the queen.

Like her.

With a gasp she scrambled back, the cocoon's sticky flesh clinging to her shoulders. Screeching like an angry wind, one queen grabbed another's arms and yanked them back. A third, red-crested queen sliced that exposed chest open like an overripe fruit. Before the body reached the ground, the red queen leaped forward, plunging her knife between her standing rival's ribs. Cheers echoed across the walls as the second body fell.

Lydele hands flew to her face. No. *Ninphor.*

One more.

The murmurs overhead had turned into a crashing wave of voices, shivering with excitement as Ninphor whirled on the arena. It took only a moment to spot her final foe, a pile of limbs not even lifted from the ground, trying to sink into the earth—

Ninphor staggered as recognition bludgeoned her. She did not move. *Lydele* did not move.

She did not look the same—none of them did. But underneath the pink and gold of her new queen's crest, it was impossible to miss Lydele's round face and lost-looking eyes. Even for a queen, she was small. She had always been so small.

Numbly, Ninphor took a step forward. There were thousands of potentials in the homeland, yet the old crone had chosen them both. Lydele flinched and shifted back against the cocoon, her knife held limply in clutching fingers. It was pathetic. A shout scratched at Ninphor's throat. *Get up!* she wanted to bark. *Get up and fight!*

They had come from the same clutch, grown up in the same sanctum, yet as Ninphor broadened Lydele never grew a scale taller after her tenth year. Ninphor had always teased her about that—*little Lydele, no taller than a tadpole.* But she made up for it in softness, goading others to her side where Ninphor had to stomp and growl. She was . . . kind. A friend. Even to someone as frightening as Ninphor.

But kindness would not kill for her. Ninphor's shadow engulfed the foolish girl as she loomed close and raised her knife. *You cannot hide from this!*

Yet the blade was heavy in Ninphor's hand. She was surprised how easy it was to drop, metal striking the sand with a muted *thump.* Lydele stared at her with those wide, wet eyes. A chuckle bubbled up in Ninphor's chest. She was a pitiful sight.

The fire drained out of Ninphor as she turned away. Craning her neck, she traced the grey-blue walls with her eyes. She looked, as much as she could, at the hidden crowd above. A shout deep inside tore at her throat like an animal. Only *their* hands would stop two from leaving alive. *Why?*

She barely flinched when the cold punched into her back.

A horrible noise spilled out of Lydele's mouth as she drove the knife into Ninphor's spine.

Ninphor—her sanctum sister, her friend, the one who always protected her—stumbled as searing liquid dripped onto Lydele's fingers. It took two hands to force the blade in deep enough the second time, and the third.

Everything in Lydele disappeared, ripped out as she pulled the blade free. Only her wail was left, shredding her from the inside.

She kept going until Ninphor's knees buckled and she collapsed without a sound. It had to end. Lydele didn't want to die here. That was all there was left of her.

The voices above burst into raucous cheers.

Ninphor gazed up from the sand, glassy-eyed and still. Lydele stared back, the wet of her eyes flowing down her face. Then she looked away, at her subjects, her mouth open wide in a violent howl.

Their new queen had been chosen.

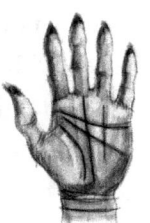

COLD READ

Mia, the fortune-teller, sat in the town square on all days, in all weather, reading palms and cards on her little table, performing small miracles. She was also the only person in the village who addressed Grandmother by name. She had been friends with my mother a long time ago and was the only person Mama spoke about with any affection.

It had been two years since my last visit, so I went to see her a few days after Grandmother had taken me back from the capital. Grandmother was out witching on the outskirts of the village and wouldn't miss me.

"Ronia!" Mia greeted me, at her usual place in the square, her arms bare despite the snow swirling around our feet. She looked as she always did, youngish and lovely. Her hair, still long and dark, was worn loose rather than bound up, the way most women her age in the village wore theirs.

"Auntie Mia," I said. It made her smile all the more brightly.

"You've gotten so big! But why aren't you smiling? Do our mountains disappoint you? Or are you too refined now for our little village? How is your mother?"

I shook my head and tugged my hood further over my face. Grandmother said I wasn't to tell anyone, and even though she didn't scare me, I didn't want to break that promise.

"Ronia? I was only teasing."

I shook my head and rubbed at my eyes.

"Oh, come now." Mia's voice grew warm and I felt even worse. "Here, I know I'm not making it better. I'll give you a fortune, okay?"

She reached out across her card table and caught my hand between both of her polished palms. Her thumbs traced the creases, making them itch.

She looked up to me. "Good news, there is a long life ahead of you, and it will be longer still after partaking of our waters. That's good, right?"

I sniffed. "You say that to all the travelers."

The corner of her mouth turned up. "Smart girl. If you're staying a while, I would be happy to show you a few tricks."

"I might be here forever. I don't have a choice."

"Oh?" Mia's smile vanished. "What happened to Sylvie?"

She looked as worried as I felt, unlike Grandmother, who had only been grave and silent when she collected me from the landlady's care.

84

"Mama killed a courtier. She's in the prison. Grandmother got me."

Mia's eyes went wide, and her hands tightened around mine.

"Oh, Ronia . . . I hadn't heard."

"It's okay. Grandmother doesn't want anyone to know."

"Of course, she doesn't," Mia muttered, scowling deeply at something I could not see. Then her eyes met mine and she softened again. "Don't worry; I'm sure they will find her innocent."

I shook my head. "It was her axe. No one else could wield it."

"Ronia, look at me."

When I refused, Mia reached across her table to gently tilt my chin until our eyes were locked.

"Your mother did not kill the courtier," she said, enunciating clearly. "She didn't, and she'll come for you soon."

Her words sunk into me, deep into my spine, knitting me stronger. Impossibly, I felt it. We were going to be together again. Mia watched my reaction closely.

"Isn't that better?" she asked.

I wanted to ask her what she meant, but I was yanked backwards by a hand grasping my hood.

"What have you done?"

Grandmother.

"What have you been telling Ronia?"

Mia looked up at my grandmother with clear eyes, but did not speak. Grandmother's scowl only grew deeper.

"Grandmother, *please.*" Grandmother listened to very few people, but sometimes I counted myself among them. "She just said Mama wasn't guilty."

"Oh?" Grandmother's voice was cold and brittle, as if just barely restraining a great rage. "Is that so?"

"Yes," said Mia, not looking away from Grandmother. "Sylvie isn't guilty, and she'll be here for Ronia soon."

"How could you?" snarled Grandmother. "You can't lie about this the way you lied about the others."

Mia's eyes glinted through the dark tangle of her hair. "How would you know if it was a lie?"

Grandmother's eyes narrowed and the air grew colder. "Oh, foolish child. You cannot twist the truth like that."

"I only want to help."

"It's *dangerous* and doesn't change the facts of what happened. I have tolerated your presence here because you have restrained yourself, but disobey me once more and you will have no home here."

With some effort, Mia stood, not looking away.

"I only wished to help Ronia. You're wrong about Sylvie. She's a good woman, just like you."

Then Mia was gone, as if dissolved into the snow.

Grandmother was still as stone, looking hard at the spot Mia had deserted. It was only when I spoke that she looked away.

"Grandmother, what did I do?"

She exhaled, her tall frame folding in on itself, and seemed more fragile.

"You did nothing. Mia had good intentions and no understanding of the situation." She straightened up and became implacable again. "You will see. Come along; let's get home."

The next day, the announcements were everywhere.

My mother's trial was moved up, for the axe had started to sing.

It sang of being an enchanted thing that bore a particular vendetta against the courtier. It had longed to slice his throat to stop his droning and had looked for the magical mind of an unsuspecting witch's daughter—my mother. Because everyone said enchantment wasn't the same as premeditation, my mother would be released. She used her bit of magic and sent me an impression through the air that very evening, promising we would be together soon.

I would have been happier, but for Grandmother, who remained quiet, her stony expression fixed on the pot smoking over the fire.

"But Mia was right," I said, leaning around her, trying to persuade her to meet my eyes. "There was something else."

"She still held that axe," said Grandmother, still without looking at me. "It speaks now, yes, but there is no magic that can compel one to kill. Mia always had a soft spot for your mother. But she can't change everything. Sylvie will fail again."

"Fail? How does Mama fail?"

But no matter how I asked, she wouldn't say more.

SOLSTICE

"What the fuck?" he gasped, sitting up slowly. He shielded his eyes from the harsh June sun, blinking away the drowsiness. Reaching up, he felt his scalp through a mop of red hair. His skull was still in one piece. But he had felt it crack like a ripe coconut when he tripped down the cliff side. He winced at the memory of his arms and legs crunching into each other on the rocks.

Then he remembered everything. That was probably the hundredth time he had died today.

The rest of his gruesome deaths hurtled back into his brain and felt like all the worst hangovers he'd ever had hitting him at once. He promptly threw up on himself.

Grant's head cleared a little and he was able to piece together why he'd fallen in the first place: the goddamn genie.

Or *djinn,* as the bastard had snapped at Grant: "The proper term for a being of my power isn't some word synonymous with a cartoon charlatan."

But Grant didn't care about semantics. The useless piece of garbage he had freed refused to award any wishes and, instead, kept killing him.

Grant stood up in a rage, kicking at rocks, yelling until his throat hurt. Then, with nothing else to do, he ripped off his shirt and threw it as far as he could. He had followed the rules: Be specific when speaking the wishes; make reasonable requests; be respectful. But it wasn't working. The genie was insane.

"Welcome back," drawled a voice behind him. Grant spun around.

"You asshole! What the hell?"

The djinn stretched muscular gray-green arms above his coiffed black hair. "Again, my name is Murad. Not a donkey's shitter." A great big yawn made his oil-slicked beard quiver. "And you wanted invincibility and the ability to relive a day and blah, blah, blah . . ."

"This is neither of those things—and you aren't supposed to be able to hurt me."

"Well, it's not like I actually pushed you off the cliff. You tripped." Murad chuckled and sighed, as if he were fondly reminiscing about a first kiss. "That was a good death."

Grant glared. "You counted to three and said if I didn't start running, you'd summon all the scorpions in the desert to sting me to death. Then you chased me off a cliff."

"I wasn't serious about the scorpions. Okay, I was a little bit. But it's been so *boring* watching you die over and over."

"Then why can't you just give me what I want?"

"Are you dumb *and* deaf? This is what you want." Murad began floating away and straight up the cliff.

"Where the hell are you going?" Grant yelled at the djinn's back.

"Back to the cave. I tire of your face flaps and the sounds they produce."

Grant scrambled up the rocks and pulled at the wispy edge of Murad's faded golden cloak. Like a hairdryer hitting a tub of water, he was instantly shocked and thrown back twenty feet, where he was impaled on a patch of cacti.

"Goddamnit," Grant said, exhaling sharply. Half of his torso was full of cactus needles, and every movement sent fresh jolts of pain throughout his body.

"You dare touch me, human?" Murad thundered. The djinn hovered above him, twice his original size. "You primitive, sniveling creature. I was about to enjoy perfectly seasoned mutton and wine older than this hellscape until you forced me here. I give you your heart's desire, and now, instead of letting me return, you whine at me."

Murad waved his hand and transported them to the mouth of the dark, dusty cave where Grant had brought the djinn to Earth.

"I gave you what you wished for; I was simply amusing myself before going home. Now I am angry. Restore the portal and let me leave this plane."

Grant sneered at Murad. While he was grateful to be free of the painful cactus needles, he was still furious about the wishes. "You want me to waste my last wish on you?"

The corners of the djinn's mouth curled into a cruel smile.

"The wishes are only a myth, fool. We acquiesce for our own pleasure. But we cannot return unless the idiot that summons us allows it." At this thought, Murad spit on the cave floor. Grant squinted at the djinn, then looked at the scattered camp gear, full of rotting books and photocopies of old scrolls. He had spent his college savings to find the ancient texts on djinn. This was his last chance to make things right.

"If I agree to send you back, will you at least fix the wishes I asked for?"

Murad spun around in a whirl of gray smoke, electrifying the air. "For the last time, human, there is no fixing something that is not broken. I looked into your heart and soul. This is what you wished for. To be punished."

The breath froze in Grant's lungs. He backed away from the djinn and slumped against the wall. No, this wasn't what he asked for. He remembered his words: "For my first wish, I want to be invincible, where nothing can hurt me. For my second wish, I want to relive a day of my choosing."

But Grant also remembered what he didn't say out loud: He wanted to relive the worst day of his life.

Snapping his eyes shut, he could still hear the cops telling him what happened because he was too drunk to recall anything.

He was driving home from the second party of the night, with his brother passed out in the back seat. He swerved into the other lane going 70 miles an hour and crashed into a woman driving home from a graveyard shift. She was a single mom with three kids.

"You know what I speak of," Murad purred, his eyes glowing the same pale gold of his gossamer cloak. "I can smell your guilt and desperation."

Grant didn't answer. The magical jackass was right. He was drunk out of his mind and barely remembered dragging himself out of the driver's seat. Both the cars immediately caught fire. When the firefighters arrived, only charred remains were left. His parents paid off the dead lady's family and buried his 17-year-old brother. He was sentenced to community service and therapy. Grant had literally gotten away with murder.

Without looking at the djinn, Grant fumbled around the cave until he found the right book and a piece of charcoal. He muttered an incantation and drew symbols on the rocky floor. As he finished, a door of blue flames sprang forth from the ground.

Murad stopped before the edge of the portal and stared at Grant for a long moment, his scornful smile gone. "Are you sure, human?"

In response, Grant sat down. Murad nodded and drifted into the door. As it closed, the blue fire grew and engulfed the cave before sinking back into the earth. Grant burned away, feeling the hundreds of deaths before and readied himself for the next thousand.

HERE COME THE BRIDES

The smoldering metal husk ground to a halt in the darkness of a violet alien forest. Smoke billowed around the man in the cockpit as he woke with a gasp. He struggled to free himself from the wounded battlemech, his coughs and cursing shattering the twilit silence. "Son of a . . ." he muttered, looking at the System Health panel on the ship's console. He hadn't spotted the hidden surface-to-air EMPs until it was too late. The rest of his unit would have neutralized the turrets by now so he could eventually take off again. But there were still the planet's monsters to contend with.

Primary battery offline.
Reroute power from shield generator.

"No problem," the man muttered. As he fumbled to release the safety harness, his dog tag twisted about and caught the evening light. The name "Private Joven Miles" flashed before he stuck it back inside his suit. With a *click*, he crawled free of the cockpit and onto one of the mech's massive arm-cannons.

"Hang tight, Bertha, ol' girl; I'll get you patched up," he said, reaching behind the pilot's seat for the emergency tool kit and sidearm. "If not, I'm sure the Brides will give us a warm welcome." The name sent a small chill down his spine that he quickly shrugged off. Joven hadn't seen them in person before, but there were plenty of stories about the man-made cyborgs that had long ago taken this planet. He had always thought the troopers' nickname for the enemy was stupid even if it did make sense. The programming instructed the Brides to hide in their surroundings on whatever world they were invading. As they lay in wait to ambush their victims, the alien vegetation would creep across their faces and bodies, creating bride-like veils. He didn't care to stick around to find out what they looked like up close.

In his camouflage suit, Joven jumped from the mech and vanished amongst the sea of glowing underbrush. As he hit the soft forest floor, he glanced at the flowery analog watch on his wrist—a gift from his little girl.

"Sunday night," Joven read, looking to the rising moon that peered through the trees. "That's just fucking great." Monday morning would be here soon. At 0600, the fleet would make the jump back to Earth, taking his only hope of escaping this losing war with them. Bertha only had enough juice to meet at the

96

rendezvous point to hitch a ride home—if he could fix her to get there. But being left behind would be the least of his problems if the Brides found him. Joven tried to push those thoughts from his mind and began working on the small energy bay at the foot of the towering mech.

The night ticked by in a series of analog beeps as the moon dipped lower in the eastern sky. Bertha's repairs were nearly complete. Joven pondered the last two red and blue cables that hung tangled at the back of the colossus' leg. His attempts to recall his training were stifled as snaps reverberated in the distance—and then, the forest came alive with sound. Faint shrieks rang out. There were only a few at first, but others steadily joined until there was a piercing chorus of inhuman howls. The distinct plinking of metal sharpening against metal echoed all around.

With shaky hands, he clipped the red cable and flipped the reboot switch. With a low roar, Bertha's system began to start up. Joven's spirits soared. But then the air erupted with the rending of gears, and the smell of smoke filled his nose.

"No!" Joven cried. He stumbled to the front of the mech and fell to his knees before the ten-ton pile of flaming scrap. His wiring mistake was clear now, but it was too late. He threw his beloved mech a quick salute before fleeing to the safety of the looming forest. Moments after he had taken cover behind a wall of purple trees, the deep boom of Bertha's explosion rattled the ground. "Yeah. They definitely heard that," he muttered.

At first light, Joven watched in horror as the Brides emerged. Their faces were veiled behind heavy vines of magenta plant-life. The visual impairment did nothing to deter the precise aim of their razor-sharp talons. One swipe and a body would hit the ground in five cleanly sliced pieces. As he watched the Brides scour the forest slashing at the underbrush hoping to meet flesh with claw, he understood how they won the planet and why the humans were losing the war.

"Come on then, you shits!" Joven barked. He fired round after round from his blaster into the growing horde. The bullets were met with a *squish* as they hit the Brides' ballistic-gel flesh.

As the machines closed in on him, Joven laughed at their pale sunken faces and brought the blaster to his temple. But only the continuous dull *click* of his empty gun echoed through the trees. The Brides emitted high-pitched laughs in return, then descended on him.

The pod door flew open and Joven sat up with a gasp. The sensory-deprivation capsule was equal parts gel and sweat as the memories of all his training failures came rushing back. The Moderator came on over the intercom, as the nodes on Joven's body faded.

Simulation failed. Surface-to-air EMP
Neutralization Mission deployment in two hours.

Likelihood of mission success: 1%

"Goddamnit," Joven grumbled, eyeing the empty pods to either side of him. With a quick glance at the countdown on his daughter's watch, he let out another curse before laying back and closing the pod door one more time.

OUTFOXED

When a king dies, the whole realm weeps. When all his kin die, it is chaos that will keep, Matrio hummed to himself over the tolling of the city bell. The midday sun was shining its brightest when he reached the summit of the cobbled road, where a small stone castle watched over the village. As he approached the guardhouse, the watchdog, a massive bloodhound, greeted him with a threatening growl.

Matrio smiled warmly at the two guards wearing the king's colors, as he did every day. He waited for the usual brightening of the rabbit's eyes and cordial greetings from the ferret, but this time the recruits' whiskers were droopy and sullen.

"Whitesnout. Basil. Good morning, my friends," Matrio cleared his throat. "The king and royal family were loved by many, and to meet a fate as cruel as poison—who would do such a thing? How is our dear prince holding up?" Not a whisker twitched as the guards' expressions remained stony and silent.

"Right, then, business as usual. I have an urgent message from the prince's uncle. I've been asked to deliver it personally into his paws."

The rabbit waved a spear towards a nearby box. "No one sees the prince now, not even you, cat. Can't be too careful. You can leave the letter there."

Matrio took a deep breath. "My fine, furry friends. It's me, your trusted royal postcat. The king depended on me to deliver his messages. Would you deny the prince an esteemed service his father had relied on for so long?"

"You heard him, kitty. Letters go in the box," the ferret screeched.

Matrio rolled his eyes and turned to the dog nearby. She gave him a curt nod, then rose onto her hind legs, towering above the guards. Confused, they cocked their heads back in unison. But before they realized what was happening, two swats of her massive paws sent a loud *thud* through the afternoon air.

"I was their lapdog for a month. All you had to do was make a couple friends," Freya grumbled in a deep, quiet voice. "That's a first for you, I know."

"You want a bone, Freya? You were just the backup plan. I swear I had those vermin eating out of my paw," Matrio chattered back. He was putting on the ferret's leather armor, struggling to adjust the uncomfortable buckles and clasps.

"Yes, well, I suppose the backup plan did the better job, no?"

He hissed at her, holding up a heavy ring of keys. "Thanks, fleabags!" He gave the bound animals a firm kick before Freya led them into the keep.

Matrio strutted through the grassy courtyard with his chest puffed out. Freya's massive form trotted along at his side. He treated the royal uniform like an invisible cloak. Only one soldier, a large badger, eyed them with indifference as they passed through the inner gate.

After entering the small keep, Matrio chuckled. "Piece of cake! See? I've got this under control." He squinted down the corridor, then whispered, "Once the prince is dead, the leaders of the Revolution are going to make us rich!" The cat gave Freya a friendly jab. "You know what, mutt? You haven't done half bad—I'm finally taking you to the Beaglesberg hideout once we are done here."

Freya gave a subtle smile of appreciation. "Beaglesberg, huh? Alright, tomcat. They're keeping the prince in the guest chamber just ahead. Fools thought it'd mix up any would-be assassins."

"Ah, now that's some fine detective work for a fledgling revolutionary."

They soon came to the great oak doorway of the bedchamber. A royal mole soldier in elaborate armor sat on a stool near the door with his head down, sleeping.

"Allow me," Freya said, snatching the keys from Matrio. Puzzled, he watched as she approached the door and fiddled with the lock.

"Freya!" Matrio hissed, almost certain the mole would awaken.

With a *click*, the door slowly creaked open. Matrio hesitantly approached.

"What?" Freya smirked. "I knew you'd fail at convincing them to let you see the prince. But apparently royal guards don't mind the taste of sleeping draught in their breakfast."

Matrio relaxed, but his fur immediately quilled up as they entered the lavish candlelit chamber. A small lump could be seen shaking underneath the bed sheets. The soft sound of Freya closing the door behind them echoed throughout the room.

"Who's there?" the fox pup squeaked as he popped his head out.

"No one, you little half-wit," Matrio snarled as he drew a large dagger from his side. "You've been quite a pain. Not sure how you dodged the poison, but it doesn't matter now."

The young kit sat frozen as Matrio approached the bed with weapon raised. He swung for a clean decapitation, but stopped as a flash of silver cut through the dark.

"What—?" the cat said. He looked down at an unfamiliar blade sticking out of his belly.

It was pulled free in an instant, just as he realized what had happened. Matrio gurgled and slumped to the floor, crimson dripping from his stomach. Freya stared down at him, a grin forming on her frothing lips.

"You—you bitch. All this time?" Matrio paused as blood burbled up his throat.

Freya smirked. "Thanks to that big mouth of yours, we know everything now. The prince appreciates your service to the kingdom." The young fox leaned into view, eyeing the growing red puddle, licking his lips. "I think it wise to turn away now, your highness," she said. But the pup kept his sharp gaze on Matrio, rubbing his paws covetously.

"You can't stop us," the cat coughed.

"Can't we?" Freya chuckled, and flicked a single gold coin onto his chest. He could just make out "For your trouble" before she lunged at his throat. Matrio heard the prince's excited clapping mingled with the sounds of his flesh tearing as his eyes dimmed.

ABOUT THE AUTHORS

Lily Prasuethsut is a jack-of-all trades and will be a master of everything one day. She has worked as a writer, editor and marketing manager for various tech websites, and short story and poetry magazines. She was also editor in chief of a Berlin travel guide and is now the founder of Minute Fiction which she is working to expand. She also dabbles in game writing, coding and watercolor while trying to write several novels that can't seem to complete themselves. When she finds a moment to relax, she can be found reading fantasy and speculative fiction of all forms, or sometimes, hiking.

Ashley Reed is a writer of fantasy and science fiction obsessed with asking questions no others dare, like "What would you do for a bear gallbladder?" and "WHAT IF PEOPLE WERE BEES?" She has worked as an editor, copywriter, junior archivist, livestreamer and game designer. After incubating in the dark forests of Oregon for twenty years, she returned to her ancestral hunting grounds of California, where she remains to this day. In her spare time she haunts mysterious basements, silent train cars, abandoned roller rinks and other odd places—all very informative for her writing.

Peter Corkey is a North Carolina native who loves the environment, sailing and retro gaming. When he's not expanding his collection of Nintendo memorabilia, he can be found watching *Game of Thrones* for the tenth time, or re-reading the series for the third time. His obsession with the fantasy genre can be traced back to his childhood where he wrote and illustrated stories inspired by the *Redwall* and *Narnia* books, as well as the Warcraft computer games. He likes to think his writing skills have improved a bit since then, and hopes to one day entertain readers with the novel he's currently working on.

Nicole Ellis is an anthropologist by training and in practice, if not by trade. She has been writing all of her life, usually rooting her worlds in the fuzzy seam where the magic and mundane tend to blend together, though she's willing to try her hand at nearly any genre. When she isn't writing, she reads eclectically, plays video games, enjoys dancing and is slowly learning how to draw again. She can usually be found in the places where stories live, like museums, theaters and book-shops.